D0295615

For Jean Pierre

Fun-to-Read Picture Books have been grouped into three approximate readability levels by Bernice and Cliff Moon. Yellow books are suitable for beginners; red books for readers acquiring first fluency; blue books for more advanced readers.

This book has been assessed as Stage 6 according to *Individualised Reading*, by Bernice and Cliff Moon, published by The Centre for the Teaching of Reading, University of Reading School of Education.

First published 1986 by
Walker Books Ltd
184-192 Drummond Street
London NW1 3HP

© 1986 Chris Riddell

First printed 1986
Printed and bound by
L.E.G.O., Vicenza, Italy

British Library Cataloguing in Publication Data
Riddell, Chris
Ben and the bear. – (Fun-to-read picture books)
I. Title   II. Series
823'.914[J]   PZ7
ISBN 0-7445-0480-5

BEN AND THE BEAR

written and illustrated by
Chris Riddell

WALKER BOOKS
LONDON

One day Ben was bored.

He put on a big winter coat.

He put on a floppy hat.

Then he set off into the snow.

After a while he met a bear.
The bear said,
'What a lovely coat.'
Ben said, 'Come home for tea.'

Some of the way
the bear carried Ben.

Some of the way
Ben tried to carry the bear.

The bear took Ben's coat.

Ben and the bear
sat down at the table.

The bear poured the tea.

Ben passed the sugar lumps.
The bear ate them all up.

They ate some bread.

And then they ate some honey.

The bear said, 'Let's dance.'
So they did.

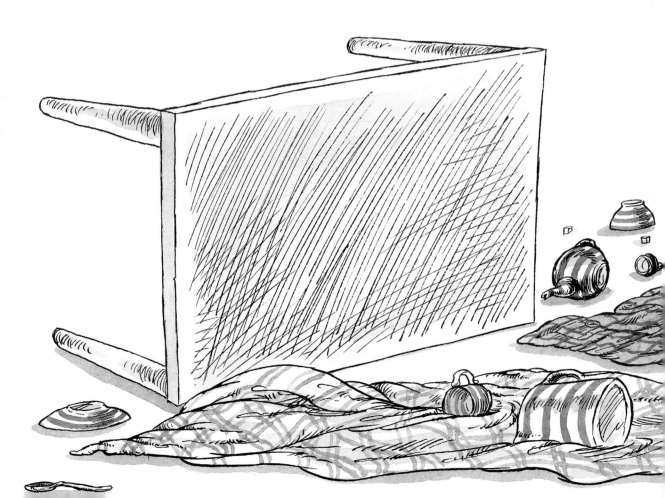

Ben said, 'What a mess!'

The bear said,

'Let's play tidying up.'

They did the washing up.

They put the dishes away.

They folded the tablecloth.

Ben said, 'That looks tidy.'
The bear said,
'What about the coat?'

Ben said,
'You can have the coat.'

The bear said, 'Tomorrow
you must come to tea
at my house.'